REMEMBERING
GRANDMOTHER'S LOVE
THROUGH HER LASTING GIFT

# Granny's Cozy Quilt of Memories

BY PAMELA KENNEDY
ILLUSTRATED BY AMY WUMMER

**gp**kids™

Nashville, Tennessee

ISBN 0-8249-5538-2

Published by GPKids
An imprint of Ideals Publications
A Guideposts Company
535 Metroplex Drive, Suite 250
Nashville, Tennessee 37211
www.idealsbooks.com

Text copyright © 2006 by Pamela Kennedy
Art copyright © 2006 by Ideals Publications

Color separations by Precision Color Graphics, Franklin, Wisconsin

Printed and bound in Italy by LEGO

Library of Congress CIP data on file

10 9 8 7 6 5 4 3 2 1

Designed by Eve DeGrie

For Anne, who continually fills my heart with lovely memories. —P.J.K.

To my friend, Rebecca, quilter of happy memories. —A.W.

# A Note to Parents
## By Vicki Wiley

We often assume that children cannot cope with death; and therefore we try to protect them from the reality of that which is a part of life. When we leave a child out of the discussions and rituals surrounding a death, however, rather than helping that child cope, we may actually be isolating him or her and allowing incorrect assumptions and unnecessary fears. By talking honestly and encouraging the child to share, you will allow him or her to discuss the loss and grieve openly.

Here are some common behaviors many grieving children exhibit, along with some ways you can help:

* The child may not believe that the death really happened and may act as though it did not. Don't be afraid to show your own sadness and talk about how much you miss the deceased, so your child will feel free to do the same. If possible, let your child "actualize" the death by attending the funeral.

* Your child may develop physical complaints, such as headaches or stomachaches. He or she may begin thumb-sucking or bed-wetting, become clingy, or even have tantrums. Be patient with these behaviors, as they will go away in time.

* There may be anger toward the person who died or toward God or someone else because the person died. Discuss with the child how much God loves us and that God is also sad when people die.

Death is a natural part of life, and the passing of a loved one can provide opportunities for families to reaffirm their love for and faith in God and each other.

---

Vicki Wiley holds a Master of Arts in Theology, with an emphasis on children in crisis, from Fuller Seminary. At present, she is Director of Children's Ministries at First Presbyterian Church in Honolulu, Hawaii.

my sat on her tire swing and twisted around and around. When the rope was tight, she lifted her feet and the tire spun in circles. Her hair whipped in the wind and everything in the yard was a swirl of colors.

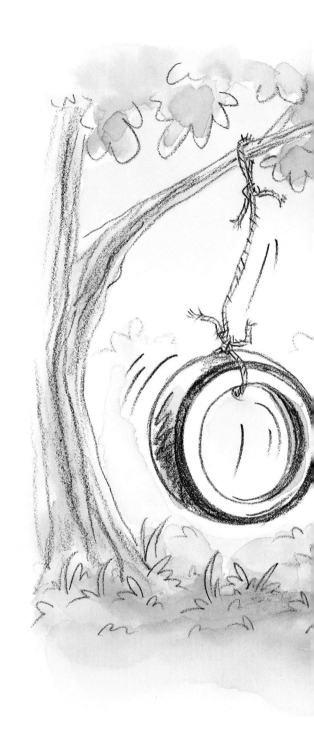

When the spinning stopped, Amy felt dizzy. She tried to walk, but she plopped down on the ground. She sat there for a minute, feeling the cool grass under her hands and feet. She remembered how Granny used to wind her up in the swing and then laugh when Amy wobbled a few steps before falling down. Amy missed hearing Granny's laugh.

Amy saw something blue in the tall grass near the fence. She crept over to it on her hands and knees. Carefully, she parted the blades of grass. It was a little bird's egg. Amy picked it up and held it in the palm of her hand. If Granny were here, Amy could take the egg to her. She would get out her book with pictures of birds and show Amy just what kind had laid the egg. And she would tell Amy how God looked after every little bird that fell, and how he loved Amy too. Amy carefully put the egg back in the tall grass. Amy missed being able to share things with Granny.

"Amy, time for dinner," Mom called. "Come in and wash your hands so you can set the table."

Amy got up and went inside. She washed her hands and made bubbles with the bar of soap. She dried her hands, then got the knives, forks, and spoons out of the drawer. She put the knife and spoon together on the right side of the place mat like Granny had taught her. She put the fork on a folded napkin on the left side. She got the plates and put them on the place mats too. She remembered some other things Granny had taught her, like how to always thank Jesus for the food they had each day and how to play hopscotch and how to make paper boats from folded newspapers. Amy sighed.

"I miss Granny," she said.

Mom came over and sat beside Amy at the table. "I miss her too," she said.

"Will Granny ever come back?" Amy asked her mother, snuggling up onto her lap.

"No, Amy. When someone dies they don't come back to us. We know Granny is in heaven now, but it's not the same as having her here with us, is it? Even though she's gone, we can still remember all the wonderful things about her. And we can remember how much she loved us too."

"I've been remembering," said Amy. "But it kind of makes me sad."

"You know, I think I have something that might make you feel better," said Mom.

"What?" asked Amy.

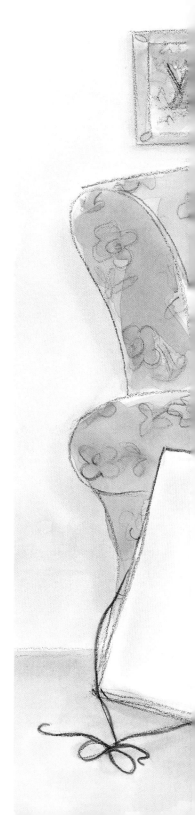

"Come on, I'll show you." Amy's mother stood up
and took Amy's hand. They walked into the living
room. "Here, sit on the couch," said Mom.

Amy scooted up on the couch while her mother
opened the big wooden trunk in the corner. She took
out a box and brought it over to the couch. When she
took off the lid and folded back layers of tissue paper,
Amy saw a colorful quilt made of lots of pieces of
fabric. The pieces were stitched together every which
way. They were all different colors.

Amy's mother opened up the quilt and laid it across her lap and across Amy's lap.

"This is a crazy quilt that Granny made. She finished it just a few months ago and told me to give it to you when I thought the time was right. I think today is the right time."

Amy touched the different pieces of material. Some were shiny, some were smooth, and others were bumpy or had patterns on them. One piece had the outline of a bird embroidered on it. The pieces were all sewn together with colored thread in different designs that looked like zigzags, feathers, bird footprints, and even a row of daisies.

"Why did Granny make this for me?" Amy asked, running her finger along a row of shiny gold stitches.

"I think it was because she wanted you to have wonderful memories of her," said Mom. "Every piece of the quilt tells a story about our family, and all the pieces are stitched together with love."

Amy looked at the quilt more
carefully. "What's the story about this
piece?" she asked, pointing to a smooth
piece of ivory satin.

"That came from Granny's wedding
dress, when she married Grandpa more
than fifty years ago." Amy tried to
imagine Granny as a bride.

"How about this one?" Amy touched a piece of material that had tiny blue and red flowers on it.

Mom smiled. "I remember that one. Granny made me a dress out of that to wear for my first day of school. It had a collar with red trim on it and I wore a red ribbon in my ponytail that day."

Amy looked at Mom. "You had a ponytail?"

"Yep. And it was even longer than yours!" Mom laughed and gave Amy's ponytail a tug.

"What about this piece?"
Amy ran her finger over a soft
piece of yellow fabric.

"That's one of my favorites,"
Mom said. "It's from the
blanket Granny made for me to
wrap you in when we brought
you home from the hospital
after you were born."

"I remember this," Mom said, pointing to a square of dark blue wool surrounded with red satin stitches.

"What was it?" Amy asked.

"It's from Granny's nurse's cape. It was dark blue and it had bright red lining. Granny used to wear it in the cold weather when she visited sick people in their homes. She brought them medicine and listened to their troubles, and many times she prayed with them to ask God for help and healing. When I was a little girl, I used to borrow it, put it on over my play clothes, and pretend I was a nurse to my dolls and stuffed animals."

"I didn't even know Granny was a nurse!" Amy exclaimed, imagining her Granny dashing out in the snow to take care of someone in need.

Amy examined the quilt more carefully.

"Hey, Mom, I know where this came from!" She pointed to a bright piece of cotton. It was green and had red and yellow apples on it.

"This is from Granny's favorite apron. She used to wear it when we made cookies together. Remember how she let me put the candy buttons on the fronts of the gingerbread boys and girls?" Amy could almost smell the spicy cookies baking.

Amy and her mother sat on the couch and talked about the stories in Granny's quilt for a long time.

"I have a good idea!" Amy said after a while.

Her mom smiled at her. "What?"

Amy stood on the couch and wrapped the quilt around her mother's shoulders. Then she sat close to her mom and pulled the edge of the quilt around her own shoulders. She leaned her head against her mother and smiled.

"Let's pretend that Granny is giving us a big hug."

And that is just what they did.

After that, every time Amy missed Granny, she'd wrap up in her quilt and think of all the memories Granny had put into it just for her. And sometimes she felt like Granny was right there with her, holding her tight and loving her just like she used to do.

# In Their Own Words

## Pamela Kennedy

I live in Hawaii with my husband and our crooked-tailed, gray-and-white cat, Gilligan. Three days a week I teach at a school for girls in Honolulu. When I'm not teaching, I write. I have loved writing stories ever since I was in elementary school. Sometimes I make up pretend adventures, and other times I write about things that have really happened to me. The idea for *Granny's Cozy Quilt of Memories* began with a special memory from my childhood. When I was a little girl, I discovered a pile of quilt squares in an old wooden chest. My mother told me she had pieced them together from the scraps of fabric left over from clothes she had made for herself and for me. It was fun hearing the story of each patch of cloth, and I thought a quilt would be a special way for Amy to remember her grandma's love. I hope you enjoy reading this story as much as I enjoyed writing it. *Aloha.* —P.J.K.

## Amy Wummer

I live in Reading, Pennsylvania, with my husband, Mark, who is also an artist. We have three children, Jesse, Maisie, and Adam. While making the pictures for *Granny's Cozy Quilt of Memories*, I remembered many happy times spent with my grandmother, Dede. Like Amy in the story, I miss my grandmother. But colorful memories of Dede are stitched together in my mind, just like the patches of fabric in the quilt Granny made. Those memories make me feel warm and loved, just like Amy when she's wrapped in her quilt. —A.W.